A Ceiling of Stars

More AG Fiction
for Older Girls

Going for Great
by Carolee Brockmann

★

A Song for Jeffrey
by Constance M. Foland

A Ceiling of Stars

Ann Howard Creel

Published by Pleasant Company Publications
©1999 by Ann Howard Creel

Visit our Web site at **www.americangirl.com**

Printed in the United States of America.
First Edition
99 00 01 02 03 04 05 RRD 10 9 8 7 6 5 4 3 2 1

The characters and events portrayed in this book are fictitious.
Any similarity to real persons, living or dead, is coincidental
and not intended by the author.

American Girl™ and AG Fiction™ are trademarks of Pleasant Company.

Editorial Development: Andrea Weiss, Michelle Watkins
Art Direction and Design: Kym Abrams
Production: Kendra Pulvermacher, Pat Tuchscherer
Cover Illustration: Paul Dolan

Library of Congress Cataloging-in-Publication Data
Creel, Ann Howard.
A ceiling of stars / by Ann Creel.
p. cm. "AG fiction."
Summary: In a series of letters and journal entries, twelve-year-old
Vivien describes being abandoned by her mother and struggling
to survive on the streets of a big city while searching for her family.
ISBN 1-56247-848-6   ISBN 1-56247-753-6 (pbk)
[1. Homeless persons Fiction. 2. Letters Fiction. 3. Diaries Fiction.]
I. Title.
PZ7.C8625Ce 1999 [Fic]—dc21 99-27129 CIP

For Kay
Together, carrying her spirit

A Ceiling of Stars

June 20, I think

To the Person Who Finds This Tent,

In case I don't come back, I wanted someone to know.

I'm going to find Mama now. I don't know what else to do. You see, she left two days ago and never came back. She went down to the city to find some work, and she was supposed to return that very same night. Only she didn't.

It's not like my Mama to break her word, and now I can't sleep for all the worries whirling around in my head.

Don't call the Social Services. Mama said they would come find me and take me away. Then she would never get to see me again and be my Mama. Besides, it's only temporary, us camping out this way. Once we were a family just like all the others. We had a house with a chain-link fence around the backyard and marigolds in the flower beds. We had a cat, a goldfish, and two cars—one for Mama and one for Daddy.

But of course, that was all before my Daddy died.

Anyway, Mama told me to stay put until she came back, but I can't wait here any longer. The people with the Winnebago are starting to stare at me, as if I have some strange beam of light shining down on top of my head, lighting me right up. I think they're going to call the Social Services. And besides, the food is gone.

If I'm not back in three days, you can have the tent. I think you'll like it. There's plenty of room on the inside, and it holds up real good in the rain and wind. Ever since we left our house in Ohio, it's been our traveling home—that's what Mama calls it. We were trying to get to Oregon. And even though we haven't made it yet, we've found some pretty good places to camp along the way. It was windy in Kansas, but before that we had some real nice weather in Illinois and Missouri.

Mama kept saying, "Just wait until you see Oregon, Viv."

My Mama loves Oregon. She went there once when she was twelve, the same age as me now, and the pictures got planted inside her head like hand-prints on wet cement. Mama says that in Oregon, waterfalls scream down mountains, and forests reach to scrape the sky.

And then there's the ocean. Mama says the sea crashes on the rocks along the shore, spraying mist everywhere and leaving behind tide pools filled with treasures. And what's more, when the waves pull back, you can see bright orange starfish hiding in all the rocks.

If I were you, I'd take the tent and go to Oregon. You can have the rest of the gear I'm leaving behind, too. I couldn't fit it all in my backpack, and there's no use letting it go to waste out here. Maybe you can go camping at the ocean, just like we were going to do.

I've got to catch a bus down to that city now and find my Mama.

Best of luck to you in your journeys. I hope you have a real nice trip, and if you ever get to Oregon, will you do something for me? Stand on that shore and, when you see the starfish, say hello for Mama and me.

Your friend,
Vivien

June 25

Dear Grandma Manelli,

I hope you get this letter, because I don't know your address. I'm putting Little Italy, New York, on the envelope and praying for some kind of miracle. Anyway, I was just hoping, since I haven't seen you since the funeral, that maybe you would like to know where I am and what I'm doing. Well, this is it. I'm here in this big city called Denver, trying to find Mama.

I know you never liked my Mama very much. Daddy used to say that the two of you saw the world through different eyes. I still remember how your face turned all stiff whenever the two of you were in the same room. Or whenever we all sat down at the supper table, how the chairs seemed to creak and the silverware clinked together real sharp-like.

Mama said it all began when Daddy changed his name. She said you and Grandpa blamed her when he decided to go from Francesco Manelli to Frank Manell. She said you accused her of taking the Italian out of him.

So it made me real happy to see you hug my Mama at Daddy's funeral. I thought that maybe we could all be a family again. I remember the fun times before Daddy died, watching football games in the basement, everybody hooting and laughing and having a real good time. But that all seems like a long time ago now.

Anyway, I wanted someone to know that I can't find Mama. She got lost after she went looking for a job. I'm real worried, Grandma. Ever since Daddy died, she's been awful sad. Sometimes she'd hold that newspaper article, the one that described the car accident, and read it over and over again. Other times, she would sit for hours and stare at nothing, holding a bottle between her knees. Once, she got so sick from the drinking that I thought I was going to have to call 911.

I thought I could find her if I came to look for her myself, but I can't.

The first night I got here, I didn't know where to go or what to do. My stomach ached from not eating, and my head was swimming like it did when I had the flu. But then I met Mags, and she let me squat with her—that's what they call it when you don't sleep in a proper house.

Anyway, we stayed inside an old warehouse down behind Civic Center Park. Mags gave me some food she had found at a pizza parlor on 17th Street. She even gave me this writing paper. Yesterday, when we went searching through the dumpsters behind the Central Library, she found a pad that had seven and a half blank pages left in it. And somebody had thrown it away!

Then the Cat Man gave me a stamp so I could mail this letter.

If you get this, Grandma, don't worry for me. Mags and the Cat Man are helping me out. They're teaching me how to stay out of trouble with the Law and showing me all kinds of ways to find food. And I took the best sleeping bag with me, so I'm always warm at night.

I'm still trying to find Mama, and Mags is helping. She knows everything about this city. "Been on the streets for seventeen years," she told me.

Mags looks like the witches in the storybooks I used to read when I was a little kid. She has long, tangled gray hair and only a few teeth left in her mouth. She talks as if she always has a frog in her throat, and her clothes are all worn out and stringy. But she wears real snakeskin cowboy boots that she's had ever since she was a young lady, and a fake fur coat with rhinestone buttons. Anyway, she isn't anything on the inside like she looks on the outside.

Mags told me that ever since she was a teenager, she never did fit in correctly with this society. But I think the problem is that she's just too kind. She carries everybody else's hurt around inside her. I can see it in her eyes—a whole world of hurt.

But Mags is smart. She has some real fascinating ideas. She thinks there's life on other planets, and that the aliens out there have been trying to communicate with us for a long time. She's been trying to break their code so she can figure out what they're saying. And then one day, after she figures it out, she plans on talking back to them. First thing she'll do is ask them to beam her up, away from this world.

She also talks about what Heaven is going to be like, and all kinds of heavy things like that. Then she looks at me and nods her head, real sad-like, and says, "We're going to find your Mama, just don't you worry about it none at all."

The Cat Man is my friend, too. Everyone calls him the Cat Man because even if he's hungry, he saves some of his food to feed the cats. When he walks down the alleyways, a bunch of skinny street cats follow behind him, meowing and sniffing at the air.

The Cat Man makes money by selling rubber-band balls. Next to cats, rubber bands are his favorite things on earth. He collects all kinds—fat ones, skinny ones, long ones, and tiny ones, in any color. Then he starts to wind them, one over another, until he has a small ball. He keeps adding more and more rubber bands until he has a great big ball. After he's finished, he usually ends up selling one of those balls to some businessman in a fancy suit. One man gave the Cat Man twenty dollars for one ball, and then he even asked for another one. Cat could have made forty dollars in one day if only he'd had another one of those rubber-band balls already finished.

There's also Skinny Willie, who only talks in rhymes, and Sergeant Sam, who thinks he's a military officer. Every day, he's talking to his troops and preparing for battle.

They're all helping me out, giving me food and putting out the word to find my Mama.

It's real interesting down here in the middle of the city. I wonder if it's like this where you live, in New York City, Grandma. Maybe someday I can come visit you there.

Here everybody's dressed up in suits and carrying leather briefcases and rushing about as if they're running late for an important appointment. When you stand on the corner waiting for the light to change, you can hear people talking in different languages. Yesterday, I saw a woman from India all wrapped up in scarves.

And there are all these big, glass-covered skyscrapers mixed in with old brick buildings and restaurants with tables out on the sidewalk. Sometimes you feel like there's nothing green left anywhere in the city because of all the concrete and metal, but then you come upon a big, open park rolled out with thick grass. There are benches to sit on under oak trees, and fat squirrels jump from one tree to another and come up to beg you for food. Men in city uniforms are always pulling the weeds out of the flower beds and picking up garbage, keeping the park real neat and clean. In the center of my favorite park is a small lake where Canada geese live in the summer.

Except for the sirens and the cold that comes during the long part of the night, it's not so bad living outside, here in the city. And as long as I'm here, I have a chance to find Mama.

So don't worry for a minute about me, Grandma. I just wanted to let you know where I was, just in case you ever wanted to know. You would hardly recognize me now, Grandma. Remember when Daddy used to say I was a big mix-up—the red hair from my Irish Mama and his darker Italian skin? Anyway, all that's still the same, but I've grown tall, almost as tall as Daddy was. Mags says I could easily pass for fifteen.

If you ever wanted to see me, you could just come on down to this city and find the Lower Downtown. Ask for Copper Top—that's what everyone calls me. I could show you around the city and take you to all the parks and the library. And then after we find Mama, maybe we could all go on to Oregon together.

I hope to see you soon, Grandma, and I hope you're doing real well.

Love,
Vivien

June 29

Dear Aunt Edith,

It's Vivien. I just wanted to tell you that you were right about my Mama.

I remember when I was just a little girl, and you and Mama got in that big fight. You were screaming at each other and pulling each other's hair, and I remember how you said that she was no good. Well, I wanted to let you know that you were right.

She left me in a campground and came to the city to find a job. Only she didn't find a job. She went out drinking instead. I've been living with some real nice people I met here on the streets, and they've been helping me to find her. We took Mama's picture, the one I had saved from Lake Powell and kept in my backpack, and we showed it all over the place.

Since then, lots of people have told us they've seen her. They've seen her sitting at the bars, wearing short dresses and drinking shots of bourbon. They've seen her dancing in the clubs and hanging out with men, too. My friend Mags calls men like that "bottom feeders"—those fish and slugs that live at the bottom of a pond, eating up all the scum no other creature would touch. "Bottom-dwelling lowlifes," Mags says.

So you were right about my Mama. She's not a good Mama, just like you said she wasn't. But I wanted to tell you something else, too. I remember when you said my Daddy was a dreamer who wouldn't amount to anything. You said he wasn't good enough for your sister, him being Italian and all.

But my Daddy would never have let this happen to me. If he were alive, he would be taking us on to Oregon and telling me all those King Arthur stories—you know, the ones about the brave knights and fair maidens who lived in a wonderful, magical place called Camelot. Did you ever know that's why I got my name? Because of those stories? It was Daddy's idea. Vivien, that's the name of the Lady of the Lake, the beautiful phantom who helped King Arthur get his enchanted sword. Did you know that?

And that's not all. My Daddy also taught me how to fish and how to ride a bicycle. And do you remember the dollhouse that I had? Daddy made it all himself, from a model kit. It was exactly like the golden castle in Camelot, and it was the best dollhouse on the whole block. All the other girls wanted one just like it, but their Daddies didn't make them one.

So you were wrong about my Daddy, Aunt Edith. I hope this letter gets to you, because I wanted you to know.

Sincerely,
Vivien

July 2

Dear Grandma Manelli,

Mama's been hanging out in the bars and dancing with bottom feeders. I guess she forgot she was somebody's Mama. Anyway, I wanted to tell you that I still haven't met up with her, and I'm still living out here on my own in this city.

But one day, as I was rounding a corner with Skinny Willie, I bumped right into a man who looked like a minister or something. He looked at me with these blazing blue eyes that reminded me of turquoise stones, and he pressed something into my hand. "No questions asked," he whispered.

I pushed myself away and ran past him. I ran so hard I left Skinny Willie clear behind. When I got to the park bench, I sat there gasping for air and trying to make my heart stop racing. Finally, I looked at the card the man with the turquoise eyes had given me:

Arch House
Shelter for Homeless and Street Youth
1270 Lincoln Street 555-0205
Open All Hours, No Questions Asked

I stared at that card while I struggled to catch my breath. Skinny Willie finally caught up to me and sat down. Looking over my shoulder, he said, "Don't trust the man, he'll put you in the can."

"The can?" I asked.

"Jail, my sweet girl, the worst place in the world."

But Mags had a different opinion. She told me I should go to this Arch House place to sleep.

Mags says it's illegal to sleep on the streets, and sooner or later, I'll get caught. "If the Law finds you, they'll take you away and lock you up," she said. Skinny Willie has been in jail so many times he can't remember. Even Mags goes to a shelter to sleep when autumn comes.

Mags says if the Police ever did catch me and found out how old I am, they would probably send me away to an orphanage or something. So now, every time I hear the sound of those sirens or see one of those cop cars, I shiver down to my shoes.

The day after I got that card, when evening came, I decided to go to the shelter and give it a try. Sergeant Sam straightened his army jacket and walked me over to Lincoln Street, just like he was sending his own kid off to war or something.

Clutching the card in my hand, I walked up to the old brick house and knocked on the door. As I was waiting, my feet started to feel real jumpy, and I was just about to bolt away from there when the door opened. Standing there was that same man, Grandma, the one with the turquoise-colored eyes. And when I looked at him, at those same eyes again, I just wasn't frightened anymore.

His name is Gabe. He has a nice deep voice and he smells like shaving cream. He's got beautiful hands—big and steady, the kind you'd trust to take out a splinter. I think he might be the most wonderful man I've met since Daddy died.

He invited me in and showed me around. Then he gave me some navy blue sweatpants, a gray sweatshirt, and thick white socks, all brand-new. He handed me a clean towel and showed me the showers. Then he said if I needed anything else, I should just ask for him by name.

And just like the card said, he didn't ask me any questions.

I stood under that running water, letting the warmth sink down deep inside me. I let it wash over me until I felt all the cold come out of my bones. I never thought taking a shower could feel so good, Grandma.

I sure hope you're getting these letters because I wanted you to know that even though I'm not with Mama anymore, I have a place to sleep now, in a real bed. Here at Arch House, they give me all the food I can eat and anything else I need, like toothbrushes and combs and shampoo. Gabe is even going to get me a new pair of shoes.

I can come and go as I wish. I can spend the day with my friends and then come back here and take one of those showers. Or I can just hang out. There's a big living room with lots of couches and chairs and a TV, and a dining room where we all eat together. The basement has some offices and meeting rooms where we can sometimes go to classes or have group discussions. Upstairs there are places to sleep, shower, and store gear, with separate areas for boys and girls.

So now, if you want to reach me, I have a real address. I'm just praying that there's a post office in Little Italy, and that someone there knows you. Take care of yourself, Grandma, and say hello to your friends in New York City for me.

Love,
Your granddaughter, Viv

July 10

Dear Editor,

Please put this personal ad in the Classified section of your newspaper. Thanks a lot.

> Lady of the Lake wants to meet Redheaded Mama. Duck Lake in City Park. Sunday, 2 P.M.

July 13

Dear Diary,

Gabe gave me some brand-new aerobic-exercise shoes. I don't know how to do aerobics, but they sure are nice shoes. He also gave me this journal to write in. "Sometimes it helps to write down your feelings," he said.

I don't really get that, about writing down your feelings, but I like the book anyway. It has pictures of flowers and angels on the front, and about a hundred clean, lined pages on the inside. It's brand-new, too.

Mama didn't show up at the lake, but that's not bothering me at all. I waited on the bench there until five o'clock, just in case she was running late. I watched a mother goose and all her babies glide by on the lake in a straight line. I stared at them floating on that lake for so long my eyes started stinging behind my lids.

But I'm OK. If Mama doesn't care about me, then I don't care about her, either.

It's just that Skinny Willie started coughing up

little bits of his lung, and he had to go to the hospital. I spent last night under the 11th Street Bridge with Mags because she was crying, and I had never seen Mags cry before. You see, she and Skinny Willie have been best friends for so long, she can't remember when they first met. Neither one of them ever sees their real families, so they just kind of adopted each other as brother and sister, and they've been that way ever since.

This morning after we woke up, I was standing in the alley stretching and I saw this real nice, new yellow taxi pull up. The guy inside offered to take me anywhere I wanted to go, so I had him drive me back here, to Arch House, for a shower and some food.

But about two blocks before we got here, he started turning around toward the backseat and looking at me. It was giving me the creeps. He had light orange hair and pasty skin, and his teeth were like pieces of dried corn. Something just told me to get out, so I jumped out of that taxi. I ran all the way to the Arch House door. Just before I went inside, I glanced back over my shoulder. I could see him at the far end of the street, slowly pulling away.

I'm pretty sure he had been following me.

July 15

Dear Diary,

Last night I dreamed about Camelot. It seemed so real to me, just like it used to when my Daddy would sit for hours and tell me all about it.

I could see the tall towers of King Arthur's castle, with their flags on top waving in the breeze. Inside I could see the great meeting hall and the knights sitting around the Round Table. Daddy told me that King Arthur put together a group of the best knights in the world, and that when they held their meetings, he always had them sit at a special round table. My Daddy really liked that part. King Arthur wanted the table to be round so that all the knights were seated equally. That way they would never fight among themselves and would always come to the aid of one another in times of danger.

In my dream, I was living in the castle of Camelot. I floated along smooth, wide hallways in long robes that draped to the floor. I had a huge canopy bed all to myself, and I ate at a long table covered with bowls of fruit and big beef roasts sitting out on silver platters.

I don't know who I was or what I was doing there, but I sure had it good in that beautiful, warm place. I knew that no matter what happened, all those knights of the Round Table would die to protect me.

When I woke up in the morning and realized it was only a dream, I didn't want to get out of my bed. The world sure isn't very much like Camelot, is it?

July 18

Dear Diary,

Sometimes when I'm here at Arch House, I like to sit at the big oak table in the dining room and listen to everybody talking.

There's Santo, a teenage kid who has spiky hair and wears army boots just like Sergeant Sam. He also wears shirts with no sleeves, even when it's cold, so everybody can see the snake tattoo on his right arm. He doesn't talk very much, but when he does, he says the F word in every breath.

Then there's Joe, who's almost eighteen. He's built like a refrigerator. He likes to sleep and tell jokes, and when he laughs, it sounds like someone tooting a horn. "Hey, girl, what you up to?" he says every time he sees me.

Martha is the woman who cooks and does the laundry. She looks like the best grandmother in the world, and she bakes real homemade bread. Another lady named Karen is some kind of counselor or something. You're supposed to go talk to her if you have a problem.

Some of the other people who work here go out every day and pass out cards, just like the one I got handed to me. They're supposed to make sure that kids on the streets know about this place. And volunteers from some of the churches help out with cooking and take turns spending the night with us.

And of course, there's Gabe.

One day, when I was sitting across from him at the table, I closed my eyes just so I could memorize every inch of his face and the sound of his voice. It's not like he's all that great looking. He's pretty old, in fact—older than my Daddy was when he died—and he wears rumpled clothes and old loafers. But whenever I'm around him, I just feel all snug inside.

All of a sudden, it got real quiet at the table.

I startled myself out of it. "What you up to, girl?" Joe asked, laughing. "You doing drugs or something?" I could feel the heat rising into my cheeks, so I just got up and left.

I don't let anyone laugh at me.

Yesterday, I told Mags about the taxi cab driver.

"That sounds like Fishbone," she said, her voice coming up all hoarse from her belly. "Stay away from him."

But later that day, when I was coming out of the bathroom behind the mini market, I saw that yellow cab out of the corner of my eye. I got away quick, just like Mags told me to. I ran and hid behind some metal trash cans that were blocking the alley.

Today, I'm confused. I don't know how writing in this journal helps people with their feelings. This seems kind of stupid, writing to nobody but yourself and all. It won't bring my Daddy back or get my Mama away from the bottle. It's not going to get me some food or money, and it won't keep Fishbone away, either.

But I guess I'll keep it because Gabe gave it to me. He touched the very thing I'm touching now. I can run my hands over the cover and know that he touched the very same spots.

I'm going to bed now, and I'm going to thank God for letting me find Arch House and especially Gabe. And even though my Daddy died, I'll tell God I'm not quite so sad anymore.

July 21

Dear Diary,

Once I heard that some people dream only in black and white, but I don't. My dreams are full of color.

Last night I dreamed that we were back at Lake Powell on vacation—me, Mama, and Daddy. We were floating in the water on those plastic blow-up rafts and watching the boats go by. We were sipping on sodas and laughing and having a real good time.

Then we were cooking our hot dogs over the fire as the sun started going down. The rocks around us turned amber pink, and the water on the lake became flat and shiny like melted silver. Sunset was always our favorite time on the lake, and we were happy.

My Daddy was laughing and talking about Camelot when, all of a sudden, he started choking. I wanted to do something, but I became paralyzed. I couldn't move at all. Mama started screaming and trying to do that Heimlich maneuver thing that saves choking people.

But I just stood there and watched.

Then it was dark and I was alone. I started seeing faces. First my Mama and my Grandma crying at the funeral. I saw them lowering my Daddy into the ground. I saw Mags and the Cat Man, and they were crying, too.

Then I saw Fishbone. He was laughing at me, laughing out loud. And in the background, I could hear Skinny Willie whispering, "Stay away, or you will pay."

So I started running. I was on a street lined with fallen-down brick buildings, abandoned warehouses, and vacant lots full of rubble. I looked around as I ran, but there wasn't one person in sight, just a bunch of broken glass and trash and a newspaper slowly blowing across the road.

I kept running, and just when my legs wouldn't go another step, I found myself standing at the campsite where Mama and I had stayed. But in the dream, we had never left. Instead, I had gone to use the campground rest room, and when I came back, everything of ours was gone. Another family was in our spot. They had a new dome-style tent and a big blue ice chest and a red checkered tablecloth spread over the picnic table. There was a mother and a father and two or three kids running around playing and all happy. But my Mama and all our stuff had vanished.

Or had I been gone so long that my Mama had finally given up and left without me? Had I spaced out and been gone a whole year or something? As I stood there all confused, a pair of birds took off right in front of me. They flapped their wings and flew into the sky. I tried to track them with my eyes, but the sun blinded me when I turned my face up to look at them.

Then I finally woke up.

Now I'm scared because I remember something Mama told me after Daddy died. She said that every time you see a bird take off, it means someone has been called to Heaven and the bird is carrying that person's soul away, just like Daddy's was when he died.

So now I'm thinking that since I saw two birds in my dream, one of them might have been for Mama. Is she dead, too?

The more I think about this, the more worried I get. In my dream, Mags and the Cat Man were crying at Daddy's funeral, but they didn't even know my Daddy. Maybe they were crying because I also lost my Mama.

After the dream, I never did fall back to sleep. I tried to close my eyes and picture myself living with Gabe in some nice house and his big hands making dinner or something. That's what I always do to make myself go to sleep. But last night, after my dream, it didn't work. I lay there for hours looking at all the shadows on the ceiling and listening to the walls groan.

Today I'm scared. I want to go see Mags and ask her if anybody has seen my Mama lately. Even if she says, "Yeah, she's been all over the bars with them lowlifes," it will make me feel better. I'm going out to find Mags and the Cat Man and see how Skinny Willie is doing. And to see if they can tell me something about my Mama.

If they can't, I won't be able to sleep tonight, even on this nice bed with all the clean covers and the foam pillow.

July 26

Dear Aunt Edith,

I thought I should write and let you know that your sister is dead. Well, I don't know for sure that she's dead, but I'm pretty sure. First I had this dream about birds taking off into the sky, and then I went downtown to ask my friends about Mama. They said nobody had seen her for a while. They said maybe she took off with one of those bottom feeders she hangs out with, but I don't think so, on account of my dream.

It's been making me crazy, so I asked Gabe how you could find out if someone died or not. He took me to this big building near the capitol. He drove me all the way there, and he just sat in the driver's seat looking straight ahead at the road, not asking me any questions. He took me to the room in the basement where they keep records of everything that happens in this county.

He got me the death records from the past few weeks, and then he just sat beside me and let me do my thing. I was holding my breath and praying real hard while I looked down that list, and God must have been listening because I never saw her name.

But I did see a Jane Doe—Gabe says that's what they put down when they don't know who the woman is. Anyway, that Jane Doe was about 35, and she was found strangled down by the river that runs through downtown.

Aunt Edith, I think that Jane Doe was my Mama.

After Gabe and I left the building, he kept looking over at me. I know he was trying to get me to talk, but I didn't say anything. I can keep from crying real easy now. Besides, with my Mama gone, I've got to be strong. I've got to take care of myself.

So far, I've been doing a pretty good job of it, too. I don't need anybody looking after me. I only wrote you because she's your sister and all. I thought you might want to know that she's gone to Heaven to be with Daddy, and you don't have to be mad at her anymore.

Your niece,
Viv

August 1

Dear Diary,

It's a strange feeling to be alone. I thought I would be sad, but I'm not. I'm not even as lonely as I was growing up, when I wished so hard for a brother or a sister.

I remember how I would go over to my friend Katie's. She lived down the block, and she had four brothers and sisters. Sometimes her Mama asked me to stay for dinner, and I remember just sitting there at their big table, listening to all those voices and the stories and the clatter of the dishes and the laughter. Her Mama was always passing dishes or wiping a rag across the baby's face, and her father was always talking about the Chicago Bulls with Katie's brother, the one who liked basketball, or telling knock-knock jokes that he had heard down at the plant.

When I was at their house, it was like being on a carousel. Everything was always moving and spinning around, and even though they were such a big family, it seemed organized in a strange sort of way, like everything just somehow worked. And it was fun. There was always somebody suggesting a game or whispering a secret or going to the kitchen to scrounge up snacks.

"I want to live with Katie," I remember telling my Mama. But she just laughed and told me I wouldn't be the center of attention anymore if I had all those brothers and sisters.

But if I had even one brother or sister, we could be together right now. We could hitchhike to Oregon, if we wanted to. But I'm too scared to go alone.

The only good thing about being alone is that nobody tells me what to do. I get up and go where I want to go. I get all the food I need at the Arch, and I always have a warm bed if I want one. But sometimes I actually prefer to stay on the streets, to sleep out under the open sky. Out there the night sky feels so big, big enough to swallow up any bad things going on in the world. And when the stars start coming out and I can see them sparkling and blinking back at me, it's better than any ceiling I've ever slept under inside a house.

Gabe keeps dropping little hints that I should go talk to Karen, the counselor lady, but he can't make me. No one can make me do anything. I'm my own person. I heard someone say that on TV once, but I never knew what it meant until now.

I like that saying. Especially in those quiet hours of the night, when I start remembering about my Mama disappearing the way she did, or about my Daddy getting killed in a wreck. I just say it over and over to myself.

I'm my own person now.

August 4

Dear Diary,

I've been wondering a lot about Camelot and why my Daddy loved all those stories about King Arthur and the knights of the Round Table.

Once Daddy told me that some people believe the King Arthur legend is just a big lie. But he didn't agree with that. He would say, "I think those people are wrong. Any story that's been around as long as Arthur's has must have some truth to it." Then he'd smile and say, "Besides, they sure are great stories."

Daddy told me all about Merlin the Magician, Arthur's friend and teacher. Merlin was Daddy's very favorite. Merlin could make just about anything magical happen.

Daddy also loved the stories about the search for the Holy Grail, the sacred cup that the Bible says Jesus drank from at the Last Supper. The search for the Grail went on for many years, and all during that time, one seat at the Round Table was held empty for the knight who found the Holy Grail and brought it back to Camelot.

My Daddy would tell me these stories while we sat outside in our lawn chairs sipping on Cokes and watching the sprinkler go back and forth.

I was only ten when Daddy died, and I didn't really understand about the car accident. I didn't understand how something could actually take somebody away for good. When I first heard about the wreck, I thought it was sort of like television or the movies, where things aren't really true, like when actors die in a show, and then before you know it, they're in another movie or something. Then, after I realized that the accident was real, I still didn't get it. I kept waiting for Merlin or somebody like him to come and cast a spell and change everything back to the way it was before. I thought that with the help of a little magic, you could undo anything you wanted to, if you didn't like it.

I remember when Aunt Edith came over and took my Mama to the funeral home so she could pick out a casket. I didn't even know what a casket was—my cousin Stephen had to explain it to me. But I didn't get to help pick out the casket, even though I would've done a good job, because they made all us kids stay behind.

While all the grown-ups were at the funeral home, I sat in my room and waited. I kept thinking this was as good a time as any for some magician like Merlin to show up.

At the funeral, I finally got to see Daddy in the casket, and that was the first time I realized he was dead. It wasn't that he looked so bad. He was lying real peaceful-like in some nice clothes, and his head rested on a satin pillow. But his face looked like it had makeup on it, and he was so quiet.

I never remember my Daddy being quiet like that.

And now I think all that King Arthur stuff was made up by somebody to sell a bunch of books. I'm sorry if my Daddy can see me writing this, and I don't want to hurt his feelings, but I just don't believe in Camelot anymore. That stuff about fancy castles and loyal knights, and especially about Merlin's magic spells—that just seems like little-kid fairy tales to me now.

August 7

Dear Diary,

Three days ago, Skinny Willie came out of the hospital. They let him go because they said he was well, but I don't believe it. He looks awful. He's even skinnier than before. Even on his face, the skin looks like it's hanging off the bones. All he says is, "That's my life, it's full of strife."

Mags is looking after him a bit, and the Cat Man is helping. I'm helping, too, when I can. At night, we're taking him to this church where they keep one of the back doors open all night just so people like us can come in out of the cold and sleep on their cushiony pews. We just couldn't stand to think about Skinny Willie, as sick as he's been, sleeping on concrete or on the ground.

Last night I asked Mags again about Mama, just in case she'd heard any news. But she said she still hasn't seen her.

I keep remembering the weirdest things, like when Mama would make pancakes for dinner instead of breakfast, just because I liked them so much, and when she would sit down on the floor and help me dress up my dolls for their dates. She showed me how to design clothes for my paper dolls, and then we would color them and cut them out real carefully.

But it doesn't matter anymore. Because I'm my own person now.

August 13

Dear Grandma Manelli,

I think Mama is dead, but I guess you don't care, seeing as you didn't like her and all. But I wanted to tell you that I'm still at Arch House, in case you wanted to know. And I wanted to tell you that I have a friend here now. A real friend.

She came here six days ago. Everyone calls her Locket because she wears a tiny locket on a chain around her neck. She has long black hair that's twisted into those ropey Rasta noodles, and she paints her fingernails with blue polish. She smokes a lot, so we're always having to go out back of the Arch so she can grab a cigarette. That's about the only thing I don't like.

We stay up every night talking about her life because it sure is interesting. She got kicked out of her house by her Mama and Stepdaddy when she was thirteen, and she's lived in eight places so far since then. She just ran away from the last home she was living in because she didn't get along with her foster parents. They got all bent out of shape whenever she ditched school, and they wanted her to quit smoking, which is something she just can't do—I already know that after only six days.

Locket is sixteen, and she has a bunch of friends all over downtown. She thinks I'm fifteen, so she tells me everything. She even started taking me down to some of her favorite places. Once we went to some guy's apartment, some guy she used to date, but now she says they're just friends. We sat on big pillows on the floor and ate Chex mix out of a plastic bag while he practiced the bass guitar.

Another time we went to a meeting in a warehouse. Everyone was sitting around in a circle with their heads all low, and incense was burning. A girl wearing black lipstick started talking about what it's like to die, and after a while Locket and I both got freaked. So we left.

Locket knows everything about the streets. She knows who's a druggie, who's in a gang, and who's OK. She knows all the stories to tell if anyone ever asks us where our parents are. If we don't feel like going back to the Arch for food, she knows how to get the leftovers off the fancy café tables in Lower Downtown.

"I can handle this." That's one of Locket's favorite things to say.

Sometimes she'll walk right up to some lady clicking down the sidewalk in her high-heeled shoes, and she'll start telling her a string of lies. Locket can even cry on command. Before I know it, that lady is coughing up some cash.

But I'm staying out of trouble, Grandma. I haven't done anything against the law, except for squatting, and the only things I've stolen were leftovers or things we found in the trash. That's not really stealing, is it?

And I wanted you to know that I'm my own person now. You don't ever need to worry about me again. Maybe when I'm rich and famous, I'll come visit you. Maybe I'll drive up in a new convertible and wear clothes I bought in stores with marble floors.

Maybe I'll see you then, Grandma.

So long,
Copper Top

August 17

Dear Diary,

Yesterday, when Locket and I were hanging around Lower Downtown, she was talking to some guys she knew and I went to find a bathroom. I was walking down behind the Chinese market in the alleyway when I saw Fishbone in his cab creeping toward me.

I started running. I ran through the garden that those earthy people planted in the vacant lot, and I climbed over the fence and headed down by the river. As I ran, my heart pounded up inside my throat.

I glanced back over my shoulder, and for a second I thought I had lost him. But a few minutes later he was cruising along the river roadway with his elbow hanging out the window and a curl of cigarette smoke drifting up in the air. I started running again, back to the center of town. I pushed past some people standing around eating hot dogs, and I nearly knocked over the microphone that one of the street guitarists was using. When I finally found Locket and her friends, I think I was getting ready to faint, because the world was becoming dark all around me.

"What's wrong?" Locket asked when she saw me.

I could barely find my voice, but finally I croaked out, "I'm OK—OK now."

Locket took me away, and we went down by the university and into that bookstore that has four levels. We found one of those fat couches to sit on. We pretended to be reading, and they let us stay there for two hours. I told her about Fishbone, and after a while I finally stopped shaking.

We didn't see Fishbone for the rest of the day. But the world still seemed dark to me. I didn't fully come out of it until this morning.

After breakfast today, Locket went to a class in one of the downstairs rooms at Arch House. It's supposed to help street kids learn how to get a job. I didn't go because I was afraid they might be able to figure out I'm only twelve. Also, I wanted to go see Mags this morning, but then I ended up being too scared to go out alone. I was afraid Fishbone would be looking for me. So I waited for Locket to get out of class so she could come with me.

When we finally went downtown, everything was cool. We listened to some band playing jazz for free out on the lawn in front of the library, and

Locket convinced a lady who was here on vacation from Texas to give us some money, enough to buy some cigarettes for her and a Coke for each of us.

But tonight, when we got back to Arch House, there he was again. He was sitting in that yellow cab, parked a few doors down from here with the engine running.

After we got inside, I asked Locket what we should do, and she just shrugged. But she talked one of the counselors into giving us a Snickers bar to share. Then she gave the whole thing to me, just to make me feel better.

So now I'm lying here in bed, and I can't sleep. Every time I start to drift off, I see his face. Then something jumps inside of me and I jolt myself wide awake, without ever moving a muscle. My chest gets tight, and my throat feels so dry I can barely swallow. It keeps happening over and over again. I think I might be having some sort of breakdown or something. I thought about waking Locket up, but she's sleeping so soundly that I don't have the heart to bother her.

I keep thinking about soldiers that go to war. I always wondered how they could sleep at night when they knew that the next day they might get killed by a grenade or hit with a bullet or something.

Now I know. I bet they didn't sleep at all, unless they were as tough as Locket. But the ones that weren't—well, I wonder if they ended up a lot like Sergeant Sam.

August 18

Dear Gabe,

I just wanted to let you know that I'm leaving and I won't be coming back. Locket and I decided this morning that we need to split. But Mama always taught me to have good manners, so I didn't want to leave without saying good-bye and thanks for all you've done for me.

I really like the clothes and the new aerobic-exercise shoes. And I'm taking my toothbrush and some toothpaste and a bottle of that herb shampoo with me in my backpack. I hope you don't mind. I took the bottle of shampoo that was already opened.

And I'm taking the journal, too.

Locket and I just have to go. You see, there's this taxi cab driver that wants to get me, and he knows where I am. Once, he drove me here—that was before I knew he was evil. And last night he followed us back here.

I just wanted to let you know, so if we come up dead, me and Locket, you'll know who did it. You can tell the Police it's a man with light orange hair who drives a yellow taxi, and everyone calls him Fishbone.

Anyway, thanks again for all you did for me. Please thank everyone else for me, too. The food was the greatest, and I'm sure going to miss the bed and the showers and the company. Being here was sort of like being at my friend Katie's house when I was a kid.

Later,
Copper Top

August 25

Dear Diary,

I've been on the run with Locket for about a week now. The first couple of days we stayed deep in the park, and at night we slept over in the warehouse. Then for a few nights we got lucky—some girls let us stay on the floor of their apartment.

One of the girls is a friend of Locket's named Felicia, and she has a job working as a waitress down at the sports bar by the stadium. Felicia sat down with us the second night we stayed there. She shook her head. "You better get yourself together, girl," she said to Locket. "Go back to school and get a job or something."

Locket was busy digging out a new pack of cigarettes from her backpack, so she just shrugged.

Felicia got up and snatched Locket's back-pack away. Then she clicked off the TV and came back and sat down right in front of us. "Listen to me, girl. Scary things are coming down out there on the streets. Something bad's going to happen one of these days, and I don't want to read about you in the paper, you hear me, girl?"

Locket was getting riled up. She found her pack of cigarettes, and then she just stared right back at Felicia. "Nothing's going to happen to us. We're looking out for each other, OK?"

Felicia shook her head. Then she got up, real sudden-like, and marched herself into the kitchen like she didn't want to look at us anymore.

Locket whispered to me later, "Don't listen to her. She always tries to scare me."

Anyway, it doesn't matter because yesterday Felicia asked us to leave. She said we were making her roommates nervous.

Last night, after Locket and I had slipped into our sleeping bags under the 11th Street Bridge, she told me how she was going to open up a dress shop one day. She's going to fill it with nothing but great-looking things, like African jewelry and long, wrinkly skirts and chunky shoes. She's going to call it Locket's Lair, and after she makes a lot of money, she's going to buy some land and raise horses.

Locket sure has a lot of great ideas. But she never got to finish that job-training class on account of me.

August 31

Dear Diary,

Locket and I have been moving all around the downtown area. We keep away from Hotel Row and the capitol, since that's where a lot of taxicabs go. We're constantly on the lookout for Fishbone.

Every day we have to find food and places to use the bathroom. One afternoon, after we had been searching through the trash cans behind a deli on Lawrence, a scrawny-looking little brown dog started following us. Locket kept trying to shoo him away, but when she wasn't looking, I'd glance back over my shoulder and cock my head at him to tell him to keep on coming. He had little ears that stuck straight up and made him look very alert, and his skinny paws clapped the concrete as he trotted along behind us.

That evening, Locket and I sat in the alley and ate almost two loaves of day-old bread that the supermarket guy had given to us. I saved some of my bread for the dog and held it out on my palm. He wolfed it down, and then he sat there on his hind legs, looking at me like he was smiling. He hasn't left us since.

I decided to name him Percival. Percival was one of the knights who searched for the Holy Grail. He was King Arthur's most loyal knight, and he never gave up on Arthur. He stuck by Arthur's side, just like that little dog sticks by ours.

Every night, Percival curls up beside me and stays there all night. I can feel the heat from his body and hear the long, deep breath that he takes as he's falling asleep. Locket, Percival, and me are always together now, sharing whatever food we can find and going to places like the park and the river. Percival keeps up with us wherever Locket and I go, and I really believe, even though he's little, that he would try to save us if something bad ever happened. Even Locket has started to like him.

Locket didn't know much of anything about Camelot, so I stayed up real late one night telling her everything I knew. I told her all about the knights of the Round Table, and about how handsome and brave the most famous knight, Lancelot, was.

Locket liked everything about the King Arthur stories, especially Sir Lancelot. She rolled on her back and studied the stars while I talked. I told her about how King Arthur brought Lancelot to court and to the Round Table, and how they became best friends. But when I got to the part about Lancelot falling in love with King Arthur's wife, Guinevere, Locket looked confused.

"They were best friends, and he cheated with the king's wife?" Locket asked, shaking her head.

I frowned. I never did get that part, either. It was so sad, two friends loving the same woman and all.

Every night, Locket and I have to find a different place to squat so the cops won't find us. If it's raining, we go into some old building, and even on the clear nights, it seems safer to sleep under some cover. But often there are some really creeped-out characters in the warehouses, and we change our minds. Then we sleep under a bridge or under some trees in the park.

We used to eat the leftovers from the fast-food joints on Broadway. But once, we saw rats running all around the trash cans in the alley, the same cans we were eating out of. We got so grossed out by those rats that we headed down to the nice part of Lower Downtown. We watched people in fancy suits set their cellular phones down on their tables and eat big bowls of salad out in the sun.

As I watched them, I wanted to dig into that food so bad that my teeth started aching.

Today it got so bad that we had to sneak into the

Mission for some food. We kept our heads low so no one would figure out we were only kids. They were serving a beef stew with corn bread, and Locket and I both ate three bowls. Then we got huge pieces of yellow cake for dessert.

I remember back when I was at home before my Daddy died, and I would beg for a snack before dinnertime. I'd say, "I'm starving."

I swear that for as long as I live, I'm never saying that again.

September 4

Dear Diary,

Yesterday I saw the Cat Man, and he told me that Sergeant Sam got put away in the mental hospital. And he said that Mags was real tired these days. Most of the time she stays in the Mission now, since the winter is coming. Then the Cat Man went off to find more rubber bands.

It's already starting to feel much colder outside. Locket says that's because we're so high up here in Denver, a mile high in the sky, and fall comes early on. I told her about the church that keeps the back door open, and about the cushiony pews inside, and we decided to go sleep there last night.

But when we got there, the door was locked. I couldn't believe it. I kept yanking hard on that door handle over and over, hoping that maybe it was just jammed real bad.

"Come on," I yelled at the door. But it never did budge.

Later we saw Santo, from Arch House. He had heard that some people came into that church one night and slashed up all the pew cushions and carved their names into the wood railings.

"They pretty much ruined the place," he told us. So the people at the church decided they better not leave their door open anymore.

Anyway, Santo is on the run again, just like us. He hung out with us for an hour or so and gave us some good tips. He said they were giving away a lot of day-old rolls and cupcakes at one of the supermarkets, and he warned us about some motorcycle cops that were hanging out on the lawn in front of the big post office. Then he took off.

Locket and I ended up sleeping in the park under a big oak tree, with moonlight streaming in between the pointed leaves.

Locket woke up in the middle of the night making sounds. At first I thought it was Percival, but he was fast asleep at my side. When I saw Locket's face, I knew something was wrong. Wet lines slid down her face and shined in the soft light of the moon. She stared forward at nothing.

I asked her what was wrong, and at first she just shook her head and said, "Nothing." But she kept sitting straight up in her sleeping bag. "Nothing," she said again.

I rolled onto my back, waiting for her to lie back down, but she didn't. I was looking at the shadows of the leaves dancing all around when she started talking, telling me about her Stepdaddy.

"As long as I can remember, he was always hitting me." Her voice sounded small, almost like a little girl's. "I can remember running away from him, trying to slip away from his hold, but most of the time I couldn't."

I rested my head on the inside of my elbow while she talked some more.

"My Mama said it wasn't fair, but she didn't do anything about it."

I took a look at Locket's face. "I just couldn't take it anymore," she said, shaking her head. Two more tears slid down her face. "I used to think it was my fault, getting hit, you know." Locket's chin jutted forward. "But it wasn't."

September 11

Dear Diary,

Yesterday we ran into Mags. She put her hand on my shoulder and whispered, "I know where your Mama is." She said that Mama was in the county hospital, sick from too much drinking.

My Mama is alive.

I thought about it all day long, and last night I couldn't go to sleep. I sat up with my sleeping bag wrapped around me, and I told Locket, "I've got to go see her."

Locket was wide awake, too. She sat up, chewed on a blue fingernail, and frowned. "It's going to be tough." She said that if anyone at the hospital figured out we were on the streets, without any Mama, they would call the Police or the Social Services.

I thought that maybe we should go right then, in the middle of the night. It seemed like a good time to sneak into a hospital. But Locket said no. She said we should go in the middle of the day instead, when everyone would be so busy they wouldn't even bother with us.

So this morning, we tied Percival to a post under the 11th Street Bridge so he wouldn't follow us. Then we walked down to Denver General Hospital, up by the emergency room entrance, because we figured that would be the busiest place in the whole hospital.

There was an ambulance parked outside the door, but nothing much seemed to be going on. The ambulance attendants were just standing around talking to a nurse. And through some automatic sliding glass doors we could spot a security guard sitting at a desk. So we waited for a long time until some other people came and went and the guard got up and slowly sauntered away. Then we went inside.

We walked directly through the emergency room waiting area to the elevators and pushed any button. When we got off, we went to the desk and asked the nurse to look up where my Mama was, but we didn't say she was my Mama. We said we had just come in from out of town to see our aunt, and our Mama was parking the car. (Locket thought that one up.)

The nurse told us Mama was in the Intensive Care Unit, and I knew that meant she was pretty sick. So Locket and I hopped the next elevator to go find her. Locket told our story again to the ICU nurse, who was a tall black man with pockmarked cheeks. He had kind eyes, and I guess he believed us because he let us go in even though it wasn't regular visiting hours yet.

He led us into this great big open room with shiny tile floors and glass walls dividing the room into sections. Each section had a bed in it, up high off the floor, with a monitor on the wall above the bed and machines making weird clicking noises off to the side. The nurse took us over to one of the beds and stopped at the foot of it.

I stood there trying to decide if that was really my Mama or not.

I stared at her face, which was all puffy and splotched with red. Her eyeballs moved softly under her lids. She lay flat on her back with her arms and legs tied at the sides of the bed.

Looking at Mama, I felt like she and I were the only ones left in the whole place. The room and everyone in it started to become blurry and fade away. Sounds seemed to come from far off, as if from down at the end of a long hallway. Even my own voice seemed to have gotten lost.

Locket was standing right next to me, but I could barely hear her when she asked the nurse, "Will she be OK?"

The nurse answered slowly, "Well, she's in DTs."

Then he explained that DTs were something like extremely bad shakes from giving up the alcohol, and that sometimes you have to get worse before you can get better. He said the doctors were giving her medicine to keep her asleep while she went through DTs.

"Yeah, but will she be OK?" Locket asked again, and I waited for what seemed like an hour until he answered.

Finally he said, "Yes." Then he looked back over his shoulder, toward the door of the ICU. "Your mother is on her way up, you said?"

Locket gave me that look that says, "Let's split."

"Y-Yeah," I choked out. "We better go find her."

We left through the emergency room, and then we ran and found Percival. We stayed under the 11th Street Bridge for an hour or so just to be sure no one was coming after us.

Now it's clear and cold. A sliver of moon is hanging like a backward *C* in the sky. I think I'll sleep real good tonight, just because I know she's alive and the nurse said she would be OK. I've got my sleeping bag tucked up under my chin and Percival pulled close to my side. And I'm thinking about those days a long time ago when Mama dressed up my dolls and how she loved talking about Oregon all the way out here in the car.

And for the first time in a long while, I'm thinking that maybe we might make it there someday. Maybe someday we'll stand on that Oregon shoreline and see the starfish in the tide pools after all.

September 13

Dear Diary,

Today it started raining, and it rained hard the whole day long. Locket and I couldn't believe how cold it got outside, so we headed over to the Central Library because we knew they wouldn't kick us out unless we did something wrong. I had to hide Percival inside my sweatshirt. But he's such a smart little dog. He just curled up against me and never barked or made one single sound. He must have known he had to stay quiet.

We hung out all day waiting for the rain to quit. We sat in the section of the library where they have just about every magazine in the world, kept real nice inside plastic covers. We flipped through the pages, looking at makeup and clothes and shoes. Every so often, we'd come across pictures of houses and families with kids and parents together, all happy and everything.

I wanted food, and I wanted to go back to the hospital and see Mama again. But Locket kept saying it was too risky. She said, "When she's out of that Intensive Care Unit, she'll go to a regular room, where she'll have a phone. Then we can call her."

Locket knows so many things.

This evening when the rain let up a bit, Locket and I went out in the drizzle down to Larimer Street. She stopped some businessman who was rushing somewhere under his umbrella, and he ended up giving us a little money. We bought one hamburger value meal to share between us and ate it underneath the bridge on Speer Boulevard, away from the rain.

Then I used a quarter from the change we had left to call the hospital information desk and find out where Mama is. She's still in the ICU.

September 16

Dear Diary,

It finally happened. I got busted.

I knew it as soon as I saw the lights skipping across the concrete bridge. There's something about the colors and the way they move that tells you right away it's a cop car. I took one look at Locket. We sprang to our feet before we could take even one breath, grabbed whatever we could, and started running.

As I ran, even though I knew that getting away was the most important thing in the world, I thought about my sleeping bag. As soon as I had learned how to squat, I learned that without your bedding, without something to keep you warm at night, you might as well just give up. I pictured my sleeping bag now, crumpled up and folded back on itself, left there under the bridge.

As I ran, my chest heaved and my heart pounded like rain on concrete. Percival was running right alongside me, struggling to keep up the pace with his short little legs.

Locket could run faster than both of us, and she was pulling ahead. I had my backpack slung over my shoulder, and as I ran it bounced up and down on my back. I tried to ignore the pain, and I hammered my feet down onto the concrete even harder to keep up. I couldn't lose her. I couldn't get caught.

Ever since we left Arch House, Locket has been the only one I've got. Skinny Willie is back in the hospital, and Mags and the Cat Man are living at the Mission because they can't stand the cold anymore. And Mama is still in the ICU, so I haven't even been able to talk to her yet.

As I kept running, I thought about Fishbone and how we've managed to stay away from him. Anytime we've seen a yellow taxi, any yellow taxi, we've made ourselves vanish into the walls of a building or become the back of a tree. We even spread the word through Santo that we were leaving town, hoping Fishbone would hear that little lie and give up on us. And it seemed to be working, although sometimes in the middle of the night, I still wake up with a start, my heart quaking.

So it didn't seem fair for us to get away from Fishbone only to get busted by the cops.

I watched Locket pull farther and farther away from me. She rounded a corner, and I couldn't see her anymore. I couldn't catch my breath, and it felt like a knife was slicing my side in two.

Then somebody grabbed me from behind, somebody big. I tried biting and scratching myself away, but it was no use. He had me, and Locket was gone. As they drove me away in the cop car, I could hear Percival barking like crazy.

So now I'm sitting in the Police Station while they decide what to do with me. They asked me my name, but I just said, "I forgot."

One of the cops laughed at me, but the other one seemed a little nicer. He said, "Well, try to remember, OK?" He shuffled some papers and stood up.

They searched through my backpack, but I have no I.D., and at least they had the decency not to read this journal. And I won't tell them about Mama. They would give me away to the Social Services, and I would never get to see her again.

Now the cops are standing around in an office, holding white Styrofoam cups full of coffee and talking about me. One of them is picking up the phone.

My legs are shaking, and there's some thick stuff starting to form in the back of my throat. I keep trying to swallow it down because I feel like I might choke on it.

Two more cops just brought in some guy wearing handcuffs, and he's all yelling and cussing and all. I can't believe it. Here I am, a criminal. My Daddy would be so sad.

If Merlin is out there, I sure wish he would show up now and do one of his magic tricks.

I just noticed that my new aerobic-exercise shoes don't look so new anymore. And my hands are starting to shake, too. I don't think I can keep on writing.

September 21

Dear Diary,

I remember sitting there in the cop station, shaking all over. I stuffed my hands into my pockets so that no one would see how scared I was.

That's when I felt it. I pulled it out.

It was the card from Arch House—the one Gabe first gave me, only now the corners were curled over and brown. The front of the card was smudged, but I could still read the numbers.

I sat there staring at that card for a long time, wondering what I should do. I got dizzy from all the questions that kept spinning around in my mind. Would I get sent away? Would anybody help me?

Then I remembered Skinny Willie's words, "Don't trust the man, he'll put you in the can."

I pictured myself getting driven away in the backseat of a long black car. I saw myself living in a building that looked like a haunted house with burglar bars on all the windows and doors. Inside, all the kids wore uniforms and had dark circles under their eyes.

I turned the card over and over in my hand, and I bit my lip so hard I could taste blood.

Then I went to the phone.

When Gabe came walking toward me, all calm and straightforward, I did something I thought I would never do, especially in the middle of a Police Station, in the middle of the night. I didn't even think it was something I still knew how to do, especially in somebody's arms.

I cried.

I started telling him all about Mama, and that I'm only twelve, and how my Daddy got killed in a car accident in Ohio, and how we were going to Oregon, but we ran out of money. He just listened to me and didn't say anything for a long time, as if what I was saying was really important. And then I cried about my dog, and I told him about how I named him Percival, and how I had to find him because I was afraid no one would feed him anymore.

He listened real hard and let me cry until my eye sockets were empty and my nose was running big-time. Then he went into that room and talked to the cops who were drinking coffee.

As I sat there waiting for Gabe, I started breathing again—I mean really, really breathing. Until then I hadn't even realized that something was wrong with my breathing, but at that moment I could tell that it hadn't been right for a long time. It felt so good just to take regular breaths again.

After a few hours, Gabe managed to get me away from the Police Station. He drove me away from there just as dawn started creeping up on the horizon. I thought he would take me straightaway to Arch House, but he didn't. Instead he took me out for breakfast and let me order whatever I wanted.

While I was eating the biggest plate of blueberry pancakes I've ever seen, Gabe told me about his wife and two sons. They have a two-story house and a dog, too, only theirs is big and golden-colored instead of small and brown like Percival.

When I'd finished eating, I sat back in the chair. My stomach was bulging from all those pancakes. I told Gabe I could fall asleep right there in the chair. So he drove me back to Arch House.

The whole way, even though my eyes stung from all that crying and no sleep, I kept scanning the streets outside my window, looking for any sign of Locket and my dog.

The next day, the Social Services came to Arch House. I screamed and called Gabe a traitor until they calmed me down. "We want to keep families together," the Social Services lady said. "We're here to help," she kept saying over and over.

Gabe helped me tell the whole story. I even told them about how I got my name and about the starfish on the rocks in Oregon.

I've spent the last two nights here at Arch House, while the Social Services lady arranges a place for me to stay with a foster family or in a group home.

I really wish I could just go home with Gabe. I wish I could just stay at his house, with him and his wife and kids.

Yesterday morning, after everybody else had left the breakfast table, I asked Gabe, "I was just wondering—do you think I could come live with you for a while?"

He waited for a few seconds. Then he said no, he was sorry, I couldn't. But he said he would make sure I got a really good place to stay, and that I could visit him here at Arch House anytime I wanted. And he said he'd come see me, too.

He smiled. "I promise."

This morning Locket finally came in. When I first saw her, she looked terrible—like a younger version of Mags. Her hair was all matted and her fingers were chafed. Big purple circles sucked in the skin under her eyes. I hugged her for as long as I could, but she just had to go inside and find that shower. She was just so cold.

Behind her, up trotted Percival, and I couldn't get enough of his puppy kisses. When the Social Services lady came later to tell me I'd be going to a group home tomorrow, I told her I wasn't budging without my dog. At first she said no, it wasn't allowed. But then Gabe talked to her, and I don't know exactly what he said, but he must have changed her mind.

"He'll probably have to sleep outside," she said.

"That's OK," I told her. "He's used to it."

So Percival and I get to stay together after all.

September 25

Dear Diary,

I've been here in this group home for three days now. On the first day, the Social Services worker and Gabe brought me over and introduced me to the people who are in charge, an older couple whose children are grown, and now they take care of six foster kids.

Here in the group home everything's OK, I guess. No one is rude or bossy to me. But for some reason, being in a real house again makes me want to see Mama even more. It's a good home, but even so, it's nothing like being in your own home.

September 28

Dear Diary,

I'm thinking about running. I'm thinking about meeting up with Locket and living on the streets again. It was cold sometimes, and often I was scared. But when I was out there, I was free to do as I pleased. Every day, I decided what I would do and what I wouldn't do.

Here in the group home, I have to follow rules, rules set up by somebody else. And I have to start school again. I've already missed the first month of classes, and I'll be behind everyone else. And I won't know anyone.

The people from the group home and Social Services are nice enough, but I don't know if I can just go back to the way things were, the way I used to be. I don't know if I can take their advice and do what they want me to do.

I don't feel like that person anymore. Maybe I can't go back to being a regular kid again.

Maybe too much has happened to me.

October 7

Dear Mama,

Since you're there in the treatment center now, they told me I could write to you. I hope you are doing fine and getting well.

I'm real sorry you have alcoholism. Sarah, my Social Services lady, told me that alcoholism is a disease and that the staff there at the treatment center are professionals who can help you deal with it.

The Social Services aren't as bad as we thought they were, Mama. They say they're going to work real hard to get us back together. For now, I'm staying at a place called a group home. Some other kids live here too, and we're all waiting for our families to get well and come back together.

It's not so bad here. I have my own bed on the top bunk, and we get good food three times a day. As long as we help with the cooking and the dishes and take out the trash and follow the rules, we get to go on field trips sometimes.

On Saturday, we drove in a big van up to the mountains, not far from where you and I camped out before you got sick. We hiked up a trail that took us up through green meadows and forests of gold and yellow aspen that shimmered in the sunlight. As we climbed higher, the trees started getting shorter and more twisted until finally, we climbed up past the point where trees can survive. Up there, the ground was rocky and covered with the tiniest plants I have ever seen.

Soon we were on top of that mountain, Mama, and it was so beautiful. Everything else in the world was below us, and I felt that if only I could reach high enough, I could grab a lift up into Heaven.

On the way down we took a different trail, and along the way I found something wonderful.

Do you remember how Daddy was always trying to describe the lake that Camelot's Vivien lived in? Remember when we went to Lake Powell, and I asked him if the lake in Camelot was like Lake Powell? I still remember the way he just shook his head and laughed. He plunked me onto his lap and said, "Nothing like this. No, this is too big and open. Vivien's lake, your lake, is still and quiet and hidden from the rest of the world."

Well, Mama, I think I found it. As we were hiking down, we passed right by it. It's a small lake, almost perfectly round in shape. Tall pine trees stand like guards along its banks. The water is smooth and deep. Near the banks, it's so clear that you can see all the way to the bottom. But in the center, it's the darkest blue I have ever seen, like a deep sapphire stone.

And while I was standing there, I had this strange feeling come over me. It's hard to describe, but I'm going to try. Suddenly everything just felt exactly right. Like I knew that I was supposed to be there at that exact moment, even though I didn't know why. I stood there on the shore of that lake for so long the others had to talk me into leaving.

Anyway, when you get out of the treatment center, maybe we can go up there together.

They're going to put me back in school soon, but for now I can catch the bus and go places during the day. Mostly I go see Locket and Gabe down at Arch House. Gabe is a worker at Arch House who is my friend now, and my best friend is Locket. Soon she'll be going to a group home, too. But we pledged that we're not going to lose each other. Not again.

For a while I thought you were dead, Mama, and I thought I was going to be an orphan. I lived on the streets, and sometimes I stayed at the shelter. I learned how to take care of myself, to find food, and to write in a journal.

I wanted you to know that I'm glad you're alive, and I don't blame you for getting sick. I'm not going to lose you, either, Mama. Maybe someday we can still make it to Oregon, just like you wanted. I still haven't forgotten about the ocean and all the starfish in the rocks, but you don't have to worry about that now. Just take care of yourself and get well.

Love,
Viv

P.S. We have a dog now. His name is Percival.

October 18

Dear Diary,

My Daddy once told me that he named me Vivien, after the Lady of the Lake, and told me all those King Arthur stories because he wanted me always to have a sense of wonder.

A sense of wonder.

When he first told me that, I think I was too young to understand what it meant. But now I think that wonder is something like hope. Hope for a better world—a world like Camelot.

Maybe even better than Camelot. A world where good people like Gabe get good things, and bad people like Fishbone get punished.

October 19

Dear Daddy,

I've been writing lots of letters, and I even started writing to myself in a journal. Today I realized something—I've written to everybody important in my life except for you.

Maybe it doesn't make sense to write to someone who's dead, but my counselor didn't think it was crazy at all. She even said it was a good idea.

Tomorrow I get to see Mama again. She's getting better from the alcoholism, and the Social Services people even helped her to get a job and an apartment. Pretty soon, I get to go live with her again.

So many new things have happened to me that I don't have time to write them all down. I have some new friends here at the group home, and I'm going to be starting school soon. I have two new best friends. One is a girl named Locket, and the other one is a nice man from Arch House named Gabe.

Tonight I went outside and sat on the porch with my dog. I named him Percival because of all the Camelot stories you used to tell me, and because he's so loyal to me. Anyway, I sat there with Percival for a long time just looking at the sky. It was black with no moon. I stared at the blackness and thought about everything that has happened, all the bad things and the good things, too.

As I was staring at the sky, I started to see something. Even in the blackest parts of the sky, in between the bright stars, in the places where I first thought there was nothing but space, I started to see something. I started to see some more stars—dim ones, but stars all the same.

It occurred to me as I sat there, watching more stars come out of hiding and sparkle in the sky, that it was like my own life. Even among the darkest days, there had been bright stars.

Mags, Gabe, Locket, Percival.

And as I sat there, looking at the stars and thinking about Heaven, I thought I saw you, Daddy. I closed my eyes and there you were.

You were wearing your armor, just like all the other knights, only yours was the finest of them all. You came sweeping into the Round Table chamber. The king and all the other knights rose to greet you as the trumpets blared. You bowed to the king and walked with those big steps of yours all around the table to the place that had been held for you for so long—the last open chair, the one saved for the best knight of them all.

I miss you, Daddy, but I'm glad you found your place in Camelot.

Love,
Vivien

November 2

Dear Diary,

Today I went back to school. Last night I was so scared about having to go to a new school, where I didn't know even one person, that I couldn't sleep again. It was almost as bad as lying awake thinking about Fishbone getting to me. Almost.

But when the first light of dawn came through the window, and all the other kids started getting up and brushing their teeth and going downstairs for cereal, I did it, too. I dressed in my new jeans and a T-shirt and pulled my hair back with a clip.

It's a big school with an auditorium and two gyms that we share with the high school next door. The teachers are pretty nice, and they even assigned a special counselor for me. I'm getting extra help in study hall to catch up on all the stuff I missed during September and October.

Nothing too bad happened today, even though I ate lunch by myself and some people talked about me. After school, while we were waiting around for the bus to come, I could see some girls out of the corner of my eye. They were the kind of girls who dress real nice and wear nail polish that matches their shoes. Anyway, I could see them whispering, glancing over and looking at me, all weird-like. Maybe they had already heard about me. Maybe they think I'm a bad kid because I lived on the streets.

I don't like it, people looking at me weird.

But I can take it. I am the Lady of the Lake, but I'm also a street girl called Copper Top, and I can find stars in any sky.

Meet the Author

Ann Howard Creel

At age 12

Today

Ann Howard Creel has enjoyed writing ever since she was a young girl. Recently she came across a poem she had written in the third grade about a man living in an alley. She was surprised to find the poem after all these years, having just written about similar characters in *A Ceiling of Stars.* Her idea for this book came after volunteering at a shelter for homeless and street youth in Denver, where she lives today. She loves the nearby mountains and makes the most of them by hiking, skiing, and snowshoeing. She is married and has three sons, two dogs, and one cat.